Bootsie

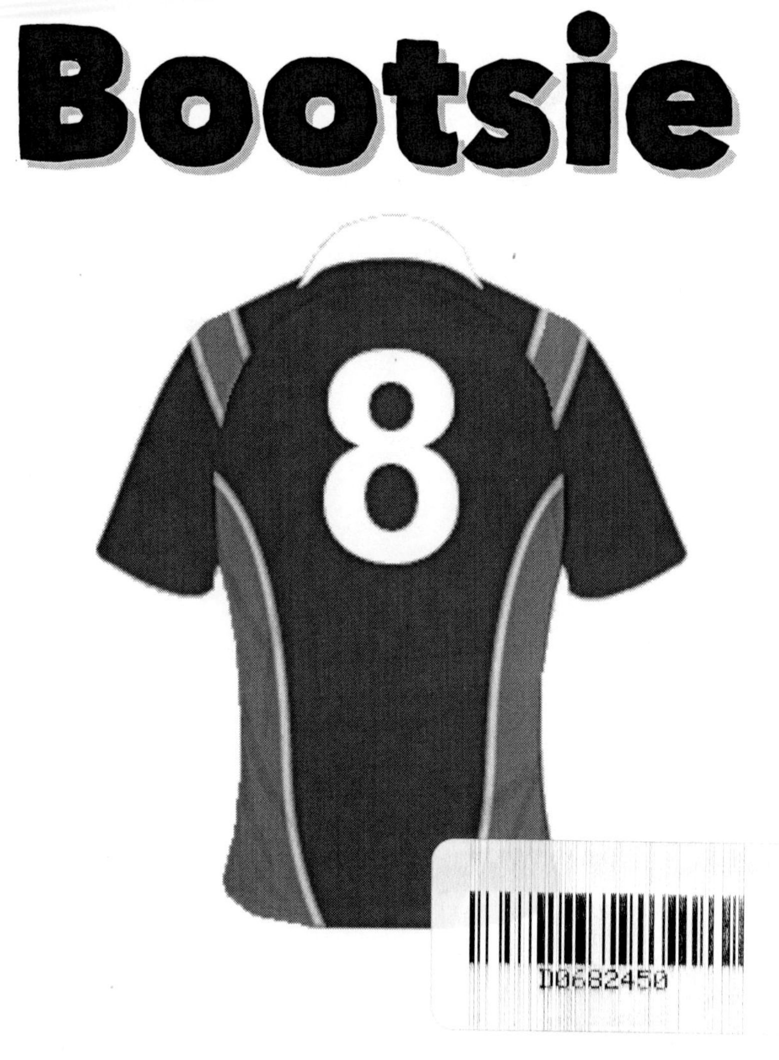

Goes on Tour

MIKE JAMES

ISBN: 9781921787805
Published by Vivid Publishing
P.O. Box 948, Fremantle
Western Australia 6959
www.vividpublishing.com.au

Chapters

1

New Beginnings

In the time it had taken for Bootsie to be able to run on his ankle again it was already a good few weeks into his end of year holidays. The winning kick he made in the final game against St David's had caused considerable damage to his already injured ankle. It also meant he had to limp around with the aid of crutches for the six weeks following the victorious game.

The sweetness of the victory numbed the pain slightly but it was an injection into his ankle at the hospital that really took away the pain that day. Finally, Bootsie was able to run pain-free on the ankle again and start to regain his fitness, which had dropped considerably during the time he was forced to rest.
"Just going to the park for a run," he said to his mum one day.
"Ok but don't be late. Your dad just

rang and said he wants everyone here when he gets home," she replied.

Bootsie went down to the local park to begin his usual training pattern that he used to keep his fitness level at the standard needed for another season of rugby at All Kings.
"Whoa, I've got more work to do than I realized," he thought to himself as he tried to regain his breath after only twenty minutes of running. He decided to take it easy for his first training session back; even Bootsie couldn't see any sense in overdoing it on day one, when he had more than three months before his first game.
"Plenty of time," he said to himself as he walked back to his house after training.

When he arrived home, his parents and sister were all sitting at the kitchen table together.

“Here he is,” said his mum as he walked in and grabbed a drink from the fridge. Bootsie took his bottle of water and sat at the table with his family.
“OK, there’s something your mum and I need to discuss with the two of you,” his dad said to Bootsie and his sister. “Actually I don’t know how to say this but here goes anyway. I’ve been offered another job within the company again and...”
“Were moving again aren’t we?” interrupted Bootsie.
“Let me finish Bootsie,” replied his dad. “As I said, I’ve been offered another job within the company and yes it means we will be moving again,” his dad replied.
“Not again!” added Bootsie.
“Let your dad finish,” said his mum who had already been told about the move the night before.

"It's only going to be for one year and then we'll come back and live here again," added his dad.
"Hang on a minute," said Bootsie, "just exactly where are we moving to?" he continued.

"Overseas," replied his dad to a very startled Bootsie.
"Overseas to another country? Are you kidding?" asked a stunned Bootsie and his sister at the same time.
"No I'm not kidding. I've been offered a spot over there for one year and then once I've been trained I'll come back and be the national manager of the company here," replied his excited dad.
"What about school?" questioned Bootsie.
"I'm sure the schools there are just as good as here," added his dad trying to make Bootsie happier about the move.

“How am I going to tell the headmaster about this?” asked a worried Bootsie.
“I’ve already arranged for the both of us to go and see him on Friday. It’ll be fine you’ll see,” added his dad to a slightly calmer Bootsie.

Friday came and a nervous Bootsie sat outside his headmaster’s office with his dad, waiting to be called. The large door leading into the office finally opened. The headmaster’s friendly expression changed to one of concern.
“What’s wrong Bootsie? You look so worried.” he said to Bootsie.
“Um well it’s about what we’re going to tell you now,” he nervously replied as they entered the room.
“Oh come on, it can’t be that bad. You’re not going to tell me you’re leaving here are you?” quizzed his headmaster.
“My dad’s got a job and we have to move to another country for one year,”

Bootsie blurted out to the headmaster.
"Overseas!" roared the headmaster in his deep voice. "What do you mean overseas?" he asked again.
"Dad's got a job overseas and we have to move there for one year," stammered Bootsie.
"You mean to say we give you a full scholarship and this is how you repay me?" said the headmaster as his face got redder.
"I'm sorry but it's not my fault," Bootsie said as he tried to explain but couldn't. The headmaster looked down his nose at Bootsie and frowned. "I'm the one who should be sorry, I'm losing my third form and junior boys captain and getting some boy from Charlton Hall to take your spot," he said. Bootsie looked up at the headmaster with a question in his eyes. The headmaster seeing Bootsie's worried face simply smiled back at him.

“Relax Bootsie its fine. Your dad rang me and already told me about the situation before you came down today. I know everything; we just thought we’d make you sweat on it a bit. No harm done,” he added as he smiled to a slightly unimpressed Bootsie. “The headmaster from Charlton Hall has also contacted me and said that he had a boy coming to this country and wanted some recommendations for good schools. When he said where the boy and his family were moving to, I told him it wasn’t overly far from here and assured him the boy could attend at All Kings. When I told him about your rugby abilities and where you would be living he said it was so close that you simply must attend his school, it’s a perfect swap. We will take fine care of their boy for the year, just as Charlton Hall will take good care of you,” he smiled again as he spoke to a more relaxed Bootsie.

"What about next year when we come back?" asked Bootsie.
"Then I'll have my fourth form number 8 back, won't I?" replied the headmaster.
"You mean I can come back after the year is over like nothing has changed?" asked an intrigued Bootsie.
"On one condition though," replied the headmaster.
"Sure anything," added Bootsie.
"When we come to Charlton Hall on our tour this year, you give us a bit of a break on the field. All Kings is coming to win, remember, and deep down you'll always be one of us," he smiled at Bootsie as he said this. Bootsie sat in silence as he thought about the situation.
"It didn't even occur to me that I will be playing for Charlton Hall against All Kings now. It seems really strange," replied Bootsie.

"Son, if any school in the world has a rugby program like ours its Charlton Hall. That school consistently produces plenty of its country's test players. You'll have to trust me on this one Bootsie, but once you get there you'll see exactly what I mean," added the headmaster.

"Before we all agree to this, there is one thing we haven't mentioned yet son," said Bootsie's dad.
"What's that?" asked Bootsie as the worried look started to return to his face.
"Charlton Hall is only for boarders. If you agree to this it will mean living in a foreign country and boarding at your new school, even though we will only live an hour's drive away," replied his dad. The headmaster interjected, "Bootsie before you even answer that, let me just say, if you want to help your chances at making it to

the top level of rugby, then Charlton Hall will push you two steps above your competition. It is a magnificent school and as for the rugby, well, it's just something you'll have to see for yourself," he said.

Bootsie looked at his dad and the headmaster.
"I don't mind. I came here for a year and it felt like a different country and it didn't kill me. I think I'll be able to handle it over there," he added.
"It's settled then," said a very excited headmaster. "I'll ring their headmaster right away and tell him he's getting the finest number 8 this school might have ever seen," he gloated. Bootsie looked over at his dad and said, "New beginnings here we come."

Charlton Hall

The time between telling the headmaster about the move and actually getting on a plane and doing it occurred a lot faster than Bootsie was ready for. In no time at all his family were packed and saying goodbyes to the family and friends who came to the airport to see them off.
"It's only a year," his tearful mum would say to anyone she hugged. "We'll be back before you know it," she would add as she wiped the tears from her cheeks.

This was the first time Bootsie had ever been on a plane and he was very excited about the flight to the new country they would soon be calling home. He *was* excited until about half way into the trip anyway, that's when the novelty wore off and the baby in the seat next to him woke up and began screaming, again! There was a brief stopover in another country to change flights and after what seemed like an eternity Bootsie and his family finally arrived at their destination.

It was very exciting arriving in a new country for Bootsie and his family, exciting and cold! Well, bone-chilling might have been a better word to describe the conditions that they faced when they stepped out from the airport to find a taxi.
"I'm freezing," Bootsie said to his parents.
"It's so cold," his mum replied, as she wiped the rain from her brow. They were soon in a taxi and heading for their new home. The house they would be living in for the next year anyway, all except Bootsie who was starting at Charlton Hall the following week. The taxi driver was full of information about the area they would be living in and answered many questions put forward by Bootsie's parents. He told

them that Charlton Hall was probably the best school in this part of the country if not the *whole* country.

The driver dropped them off at the new house in Charlton. He wished the family well during their stay in their adopted country and good luck to Bootsie with his rugby at Charlton Hall.

The house was built around the start of the 1800's and it looked like it had been built for royalty. It had high ceilings with huge chandeliers hanging in most of the rooms. All the furniture looked like antiques and would be very expensive to replace.
"No rugby in here, Bootsie," his mum said to him as she examined a very large ceramic vase.

For the next few days the family took in the local area. They went on sightseeing trips to check out where they would be calling home for the next year. It wasn't long before Sunday morning came and Bootsie had to pack again and get ready for his new school. His parents had become friends with their new neighbours who offered them the use of their car to drive down to Charlton Hall with Bootsie. As they drove along what seemed like a never-ending entrance road into the school, they couldn't help but be amazed by the school grounds.

"It's all so green," his mum said as she looked out of the car window. "Pretty impressive," his dad replied.

"I thought All Kings was something," added Bootsie from the back seat, "but this place is, well I can't even find a word for it."

They eventually arrived at the main buildings of the school and were greeted by a man in a red jacket who

opened the door for Bootsie's mum.
"Good morning," he said with a smile.
"Welcome to Charlton Hall," he added.
"Are you the headmaster?" asked Bootsie. The man chuckled, "Oh' no son, I'm not the headmaster. He is expecting you though," he added. He led them into one of the main halls of the building and through to the headmaster's office.
"He'll be out in a moment," he said, as he wished them well and returned outside. Not long after, the door opened and they were greeted by the headmaster.
"Welcome, welcome" he said in a loud voice. "We've been expecting you young man. And how was the plane trip here?" he asked Bootsie's parents.
"Long," his dad replied with a smile. Bootsie was soon made aware of what was expected of him during his stay at the school and if he thought All Kings was strict then he was in for a rude

welcome at Charlton Hall. The book of guidelines was twice as thick as the one from All Kings.

There was a knock at the door and one of the dormitory masters Mr Shepherd greeted Bootsie and his family and told them he would soon show Bootsie to his dormitory. As they stood outside the headmaster's office, Mr Shepherd shocked Bootsie when he told him he would have to say goodbye to his parents, as only students and staff were permitted to enter the dormitories.
"Oh. Okay then," he said.
"Don't worry dear you'll be fine here and in no time you will make some new friends," said his mum as she hugged him goodbye.
"Chin up son we'll be at your game each week," added his dad.
"Its fine. I've done this before," he replied to his parents, "don't worry about me I'll fit in."

Bootsie waved goodbye to his parents before walking away from the main building.
"C'mon young man let's get you settled in," said Mr Shepherd as he patted Bootsie on the back.

"You must be very special if the head-master wanted to meet you in person," he said to Bootsie as they walked the short distance to the dormitories.
"I don't know about that," he replied.
"This is your dormitory, Bootsie," said Mr Shepherd as he ushered Bootsie into one of the buildings.
"Cullen. It's a dormitory for third formers. I live in the small room at the end of the corridor just over there so I will be keeping an eye on what goes on in here," he said to Bootsie as he put his bags down next to his bed.
"Where is everyone?" asked Bootsie.
"Give it time. This place will slowly fill up today and by the evening meal

we'll have a full house," he replied. Mr Shepherd wished him well and returned to his own room at the end of the corridor.

Bootsie began to unpack his belongings and make himself at home in his new cubicle, which was much bigger than the one he had at All Kings. His uniform had already been placed inside his wardrobe and was hanging in plastic bags all neatly ironed and ready to wear. He took out the blazer and had a look at it. The blazer was black with narrow red piping around the front of the collar and on the bottom of the sleeves. The school shield was sown onto the top left, front pocket. It was a white shield with a blue cross and in the middle of it were the words *Fortis est veritas* and *1874* written into the cross. The school was built in 1874 and Fortis est veritas was the school's motto in

Latin which meant 'Truth is strong'.
"I can't believe I'm at Charlton Hall," Bootsie said to himself as he looked down at the blazer.

"Haven't seen you here before," a voice from behind said. Bootsie turned around to see a boy standing behind him carrying a lot of bags and a blazer the same as the one he was holding.
"No, I'm new here," said Bootsie.
"With that accent I don't think you're just new to the school either," the boy replied. Bootsie chuckled as he explained why he was at the school.
"The name's Harry. *Headline Harry* they call me around here," said the boy as he dropped most of his bags and put his hand out for a handshake.
"Bootsie," replied Bootsie.
"Unusual name," replied Harry, "I'm the head journalist for the school's paper,' he added. "Do you write?"
"Um no. No I don't," replied Bootsie.

"What do you do then?" asked Harry.
"Um play rugby hopefully," replied Bootsie.
"Oh, a rugby player," groaned Harry, "and here was me starting to think you were normal," he sighed, and with that he simply picked up his bags again and began to walk away. After only a short distance Harry looked back at Bootsie with a smirk on his face and said, "Let's just say that the rugby players and the press don't have the best of relationships here." "Boy journalists, more boy journalists," Bootsie thought to himself as he put his blazer back into the wardrobe, "I guess some things are the same the world over."

The Complete History of
Charlton Hall Rugby
Charlton Hall
Fortis est veritas
1
8
7
4
Rugby Union

Charlie

Mr Shepherd was right about one thing. By the start of the evening meal, Charlton Hall was a full house. The school had nearly twice as many students as All Kings and to cater for this everything was bigger, including the dining hall. The boy Bootsie sat next to was full of information about the school and had been a boarder since he was very young. His name was Charles but introduced himself as Charlie.

"Whatever you want to know about the school I'm your man," he said with a smile. "That's the rugby boys over on that table there and over on that other table are their arch enemies the paper boys as I like to call them," he added as he pointed to each group.
"I call them boy journalists," replied Bootsie. Bootsie listened on with interest as Charlie filled him in on the

relationship between the rugby boys and the paper boys.
"Rugby is pretty big here, I don't know how much you know about the game but around here it's like a religion," he said.

Bootsie soon realised that the rugby boys were all sitting at two large tables to one side of the hall and there was no spare seat for him at the table. He couldn't work out if they were junior boys or senior boys as they all seemed very big. Charlie began to tell Bootsie a few things about rugby at Charlton Hall.
"The rugby boys are like gods at this school and get treated extremely well. They go on tours around the country to play against other schools as well as overseas trips to do the same. There's a school coming to play here this year called All Kings. Our team taught

them a rugby lesson when they met on last year's overseas trip."
Bootsie just smiled and nodded and took all the information on board without mentioning anything about the game, All Kings or rugby at all.

Bootsie continued to play the same card and just listened and said things like, "Uh huh and oh, okay," in response to what Charlie was telling him.
"The rugby boys are very well respected here, if you could get on one of the teams and sit at those tables, people would really know who you are around here," said Charlie, "I've been here for ever and I think most people here don't even know my name," he added.
"Well Charlie, *I* know your name and I've only been here for a few hours," replied Bootsie with a smile.

This one small comment really made Charlie happy; it also made him talk even more. So much so, that once he started Bootsie couldn't stop him, Charlie gave Bootsie what might have been the entire history of Charlton Hall during the evening mealtime. It didn't stop then either. Charlie happened to be in the same dormitory as Bootsie and he made himself at home on the end of Bootsie's bed when they returned from the dining hall.

"This kid could talk underwater," Bootsie thought to himself as Charlie continued the history lesson. He talked about the school, the rugby boys, the school, the rugby boys, the school and the rugby boys always in the same order one after the other. Charlie showed Bootsie his wardrobe which was full of previous editions of the school newspaper; he was a walking encyclopedia when it came to rugby at Charlton Hall. Charlie knew every player who played and had ever played at the school now and from the last twenty years. Bootsie was filled in on most of them, as well as any test player who had been a student at Charlton Hall and had gone on to make it at the top level.

Although Charlie did most of the talking, well *all* of the talking, it did fill Bootsie in on what he was up against if he wanted to make the team, which he did. Mr Shepherd came down and told the boys that supper was ready and they had half an hour after supper until lights out. Charlie continued the lesson as they walked to the supper table which was set up outside the dining hall and was full of big silver pots full of steaming hot tea and hot chocolate. As they stood in the queue to get served, Charlie didn't stop for air once. He kept on and on about how huge rugby was at the school and how he wished he could be a rugby boy or even be friends with the rugby boys.

Bootsie still listened to every word he was being told but as he poured the tea into his cup, the aroma of the tea reminded him of Syd's house. He remembered how Syd would fill him with advice about life and how to deal with certain things and certain people, all while his wife filled him with tea and chocolate biscuits that she had made. Bootsie must have switched off from Charlie while he thought about Syd because all of a sudden Charlie went quiet and Bootsie didn't know why.

"Are you OK?" he asked a very silent Charlie.

"That, that, that's the captain of the school and more importantly the captain of the senior boy's team," he

said as he pointed to a particular boy who was filling his cup from one of the teapots.
"So?" said Bootsie, "He's just a boy," he added.
"Not around here he's not," replied Charlie as he looked on in awe of the boy. "Around here he's like a god," he continued.

Bootsie and Charlie sat on a small brick wall and drank their tea; Charlie would point out to Bootsie every time a rugby boy came up to the supper table. Charlie soon taught Bootsie who each and every player in the junior team and senior teams were and what position they played. Bootsie was very interested in the junior boys' number 8 as it was the spot on the team he wanted. His surname was Oxlander but according to Charlie he was known only as 'Ox'.

"Everyone calls him Ox," he said to Bootsie who couldn't stop staring at the boy.
"Big boy," he said to Charlie. "Are you sure he's not a senior boy?" asked Bootsie.
"Nope, he's our junior number 8," Charlie replied.
"The boy's a monster!" Bootsie secretly thought to himself as he watched Ox return to the dormitory with his cup in hand.

Bootsie finished the last of his tea and returned to the dormitory with Charlie still in tow. Bootsie certainly had made a new friend in Charlie even though he was like the small fish that hangs around a shark and never leaves its side. For the next few weeks Charlie was the small fish and Bootsie was the shark. Every time Bootsie turned around Charlie was behind him, like a shadow. He also noticed that he was the only person Charlie followed around. In all the years he had been at Charlton Hall, Bootsie was the only friend that Charlie had ever made. Maybe it was the fact that Charlie never stopped talking, especially about rugby that eventually drove people away. Even *he* wasn't sure, but in Bootsie he had finally found his first friend. Although others may have found Charlie annoying, Bootsie thought he was great. At times he had to tell him enough was enough but on the whole he had really grown on Bootsie. Charlie had also really helped Bootsie out during his first few months at Charlton Hall and it certainly made settling into a new school in a new country a lot easier for him and being a friend to Charlie was the least Bootsie could do.

Bootsie knew that the first night of training was nearing and soon he would have to tell Charlie his secret about playing rugby, he had kept it to himself as he knew that once he told Charlie he was here to play rugby there would be no letting up from him. Charlie worshipped the rugby boys and once Bootsie told him he was going to try out for the team it was just as he had expected. Charlie was stunned with the news; it was the first time since Bootsie had sat next to him at the dining hall on the first night that Charlie didn't speak for more than ten minutes.

"My friend is going to be on the rugby team," he eventually said to Bootsie.
"Hang on I've got to get on the team first," replied Bootsie.
"I've got a friend on the rugby team," he added as he walked away from

Bootsie like a zombie and back to his own cubicle.
"Wait Charlie, I'm not in there yet," Bootsie shouted to him, but Charlie didn't hear him he just kept mumbling to himself, "I've got a friend on the rugby team," over and over again. Bootsie lay back on his bed and said to himself, "I'm not there yet, and I won't be there if Ox has anything to do with it either."

Once Bootsie knew what he was up against in Ox he couldn't stop watching him around the school. He was a huge boy and looked like he was a good few years older than most of the other third formers. He was in one of Bootsie's classes and he had to sit in the back row because he was so big, anyone who sat behind him had no chance of seeing the teacher at the front of the class. He may have been big but one thing he *did* miss out on was brains. Unfortunately for Ox he was used as a target for many people's jokes usually at his expense of course, but he either didn't get it or didn't care about it because Bootsie never saw him get mad once. Bootsie would soon realize the hard way that Ox did get mad about the jokes made about him and he had his own way of dealing with it. On the rugby field!

4

The Ox

Bootsie finally got to lace up his boots for the first night of training. He walked down to the training fields with Charlie right behind him.
"Can I carry your bag?" asked Charlie.
"No Charlie, I can carry it myself," replied Bootsie, as he reached into his bag and handed Charlie his black scrum cap.
"Here, you can wear this until we get to training," he added.
Charlie was very pleased and ran on in front with the scrum cap on his head and the ball that he always kept in his cubicle under his arm.
"Nice sidestep!" Bootsie shouted to him.
"My Dad taught me," he shouted back as he began sidestepping all the light poles along one of the paths that led down to the rugby fields.

Bootsie joined the rest of the boys on the field who were hanging around waiting for the coach to arrive while Charlie went and sat in the grandstand. Bootsie stood next to the boys but felt very out of place as he didn't know anyone on the teams at all. One boy came over to him and shocked Bootsie when he asked if Bootsie remembered him.

"No, I'm new here I don't know anyone," Bootsie replied.

"Surely you remember me?" the boy asked, "All Kings last year. You were the number 8 weren't you? We swapped jumpers after the game," he added. Bootsie was stunned.

"Yes that was me," he said to the boy with a smile, "It was pretty muddy though, remember?" Bootsie added.

"Hey guys, do you know who this boy is?" he said to the group.

"Yeah who?" asked one of the boys.

"All Kings number 8 last year from the tour," he told the group.

Bootsie cringed as the big Ox looked over at him. He didn't say anything but by the way he looked at Bootsie he didn't have to, he got the message loud and clear.

The boys slowly introduced themselves until the coach arrived and spoke to the group.
"Evening boys, welcome to day one," he said to the combined junior and senior boys team who were gathered in front of him.
"Here's hoping we have a better year this season than last hey, although you junior boys can't get any worse than last place can you?" he sarcastically said to the boys.
"Last place," Bootsie thought to himself. Charlie hadn't told him that Charlton Hall's junior boys had finished in last place in the competition for the first time since the school had opened in 1874. The senior boys had

come second and missed out on the shield by a point.
"Pressure's off me a bit anyway," Bootsie also thought as he stood there and listened to the coach. He was even more pleased when he heard the coach say fresh blood might be the way to get them back into winning form.

If it was the fact they had finished bottom last year or this was always how training was, then the coach had a pretty physical approach when it came to training. Bootsie had made the mistake of wearing his new boots to training for the first time without wearing them in beforehand. He could feel them rubbing and a blister forming on his heel where his sock had a hole in it. Something else wasn't right either and he just couldn't put his finger on it. When he ran, it just didn't feel right. The coach knew

about Bootsie and put him to work with the forwards, although the head coach was the backs coach and the forwards had a different coach to help them.
"A coach and an assistant coach. Unreal," Bootsie thought to himself.

By no means were these boys unfit either. Sure, this was the first night of training and fitness levels would improve as the season went on, but for day one Bootsie found himself a little behind. He quickly learnt one thing about the Ox. The boy was good. For such a big unit he could really move, he was easily four to five inches taller than Bootsie, a fair bit heavier too and his strength was incredible. Bootsie immediately knew he was going to have his work cut out for him trying to crack into this team.

Bootsie had one opportunity. The boy with whom he had swapped jumpers after the All Kings game wanted the number 7 openside flanker spot this season. He'd laughed when he told Bootsie that he was welcome to the number 8 jumper if he could beat Ox for the spot. Apart from feeling a little bit unfit, Bootsie was putting on a good display for his new coach but couldn't help feeling that the ground seemed quite hard every time he was tackled and hit the deck. He had a great run up field when he picked the ball up from behind a ruck but was soon mowed down by another player who drilled him into the ground and ripped the ball from his grasp. Bootsie sat up and was seeing stars for the first time since he had pulled on a Bulldogs jumper when he was six.

“What was that?” he thought to himself as he sat trying to regain his senses. He heard a muffled voice say something to him; he looked up and could see the Ox standing over him.
“What did you say?” asked a confused Bootsie. Ox reached into his own mouth and pulled out his mouth guard, and a big dribble of his spit trickled out of his mouth and hit Bootsie in his face.
“I said you should wear a scrum cap to protect your head,” he said in a deeper voice than most men would like to have.
“A what?” a dazed Bootsie asked. Ox patted him on the head, “Scrum cap. Get one. Protect your brain,” added Ox as he ran away.

Bootsie looked over at Charlie sitting in the stand and realized he was still wearing his scrum cap.

"No wonder the ground seemed harder," he thought as he regathered himself. The coach came over to see if he was all right.
"You okay son?" he asked Bootsie.
"I think so," he replied.
"Have you met Ox before?" the coach asked Bootsie.
"Only in class," was all Bootsie could squeeze out.
"That boy will play test rugby for this country one day you mark my words," added the coach, "Go take a breather for a second, get some air back," he continued.
"No I'm fine. I've been hit harder than that before," replied Bootsie. "Yeah. Did you get hit by a rhino once, did you?" laughed the coach as he walked away.
"No but I think I just might have," he thought to himself as he walked over to the grandstand to get his scrum

cap back from Charlie and sucking in as much air as his crushed lungs would allow.

“Ooh that must have hurt,” remarked a sympathetic Charlie.
“Nah, I’m okay,” said Bootsie, trying to cover the fact he had just been hit harder than he had ever been hit before.
“The coach reckons Ox will play test rugby for this country one day” said Charlie to an unimpressed Bootsie.
“The boy hits hard,” was all Bootsie added to the suggestion. The hit from Ox had come right at the end of training and by the time Bootsie had grabbed his scrum cap from Charlie, the coach had called them in for a meeting on the side line.
“Not bad boys, for day one, but just remember we’re at the bottom of the mountain and were just getting our gear ready to climb the mountain.

Next session we'll put on our gear and start the climb and we won't stop climbing until we get to the top this year. OK?" he said to the group. "Not bad for day one," thought Bootsie as he held onto his aching ribs. "How bad is this going to get?"

Sometimes it's nicer when you don't know what's in front of you otherwise you might not want to get out of bed to face it. Luckily for Bootsie he didn't know yet what was in store for him, even before the season had started. If he had known what he was about to face he probably would have stayed in bed instead.

5 Pain

Staying in bed after he woke up the next morning would have been a nice option for Bootsie. The sound that came out of Bootsie's mouth when he tried to get out of bed doesn't have a word that could describe it but anyone hearing it would know someone was in agony. After a painful trip to the bathroom, he carefully made his way into the dining hall and sat next to Charlie.

"Well, well. How is the rugby boy this morning?" asked Charlie in an excited voice which would have been nice, except he nudged Bootsie in his ribs with his elbow as he asked.

"Uugh," was the reply that came out of Bootsie.

"Oh sorry. Are you okay?" asked Charlie.

"It's nothing," replied Bootsie, trying to mask the pain as he noticed that Ox was looking over at him and had given him a cheerful nod. Bootsie ignored what he really felt and gave him the same friendly nod back.

The Charlton Hall rugby team trained on Tuesdays and Thursdays and for poor Bootsie it had been only two nights since he had felt the boy mountain Ox smash him into the ground at the team's first training session on Tuesday. To say he wasn't quite ready by Thursday was an understatement. The coach had designed a cross-country run for the group. The route was punishing to say the least. Charlton Hall was surrounded by very thick forest. There were also many large lakes within the grounds that the boys had to swim across before continuing their run.

Bootsie's ribs were so sore that every time he took a deep breath he thought he would pass out from the pain. The run was extremely hard and Bootsie

was taking plenty of deep breaths. He managed to complete the course even though he wasn't anywhere near the first group of boys who had already finished and were waiting with the coach. When the last of the boys arrived, the coach addressed them all. "Good effort from everyone tonight and it's what I want to see for the rest of the season from you as well," he said. "Now off you go and we'll meet in the gym for a weights session first thing on Saturday morning followed by an afternoon track session," he added.
"Weights, afternoon track session," Bootsie thought to himself as he dragged himself to the dormitory for a shower. As he stood under the hot water it suddenly dawned on him that *he* was paying for *their* poor performance in the competition last year.

Saturday morning came and Charlie went with Bootsie to the gym, which had a full, state-of-the-art weights training section that could put any commercial gym to shame. Bootsie had never been a big fan of weights but at this school if you wanted to play rugby you had to train in the gym. One thing that did amaze him was how much some of the other boys could lift; Ox could bench press three times what Bootsie could press. When it came to squats Bootsie was also way behind. It had been over a year since he had ridden to the Hornets training, up all the big hills each week and it was showing a bit.

"Have I gone a bit soft since I've been at All Kings?" he asked himself in the gym. "I don't feel like I have," he thought. For the rest of the session he did what he felt comfortable with, but vowed to himself that he would visit the gym as often as he could, before and during the season.

If the gym session in the morning was painful, then the afternoon track session was the icing on the cake, the pain cake. The coach had some small metal sleds, each with a short pole in the middle over which steel weights from the gym could be slid. Each boy had to put on a wide leather belt that was joined to a sled by a length of thick elastic. After only a few of the sled runs, Bootsie's leg muscles felt like they were on fire and by the end of the session Bootsie was so exhausted, he *had* to let Charlie carry his bag for him.

This sort of training was how it was at Charlton Hall and over the next few weeks Bootsie made another friend at the school; his new friend was 'pain'. Bootsie dragged Charlie to the gym each time he went there and Charlie soon became his full-time training partner. He loved anything to do with helping Bootsie or any of the other rugby boys, and because of his friendship with Bootsie, soon became a part of the rugby group. None of the rugby boys would have ever known Charlie if Bootsie hadn't befriended him and soon enough he was a good team player to have around. Most of the rugby boys now knew him by name and Charlie loved it, he was even starting to build up a decent physique for himself as he was training nearly every day with Bootsie.

When Bootsie wasn't in the gym, he would grab a sled from the sports shed and train with it. Even Charlie would pull a sled as well. They would also get up most mornings and do a smaller version of the cross-country run together before breakfast. Charlie no longer sat in the stands and watched at training either; he would run water out to the players and loved his new role within the team. He even had to send a letter to his parents asking for new shorts, as his newly muscled legs made the old ones feel too tight.

The last Thursday before the first game of the season soon came and the coach went a lot easier on the boys he had moulded since the first training session many weeks ago.
"Are we ready?" he asked the group, as they gathered round at the end of training.
"Yes," responded the boys, almost in a whisper.
"Pathetic. I said *are we ready*?" he asked again. This time he got the response he was looking for.
"*YES*!" the boys screamed as one.
"That's better. It's the opening game of the season on Saturday and we are

going to start with a win and I won't accept anything else but that.
If any teams this year have worked as hard as we have pre season then it will tell on the field. But you mark my words, come Saturday, our efforts so far will pay off," he said to the boys. "It was a disgrace and an embarrassment for this school to come where it did last year and most of you boys were a part of it. Just let me tell you that this year is going to be a complete turnaround. We're going from last to first all in the space of one season. No questions asked and let me also say that when those pompous All Kings boys get here in a few weeks, we are going to make them wish they had stayed home," he added with a snarl.
"Ouch!" thought Bootsie. "Pompous All Kings boys. That hurts," he thought to himself as he put his hands into the middle of the huddle.

Talk about feeling in limbo, he wanted to go out and win for his new school on Saturday, but the pompous All Kings comment really startled him. Deep down Bootsie was still an All King, and Charlton Hall was just a temporary thing and he knew he would be leaving at the end of the year regardless of where they finished in the competition.

"Pompous All Kings boys," he said over and over to himself as he walked back to the dormitory. The comment had really cut him and to make matters worse he would have to play against his own real school in a few weeks when they arrived in the country. The whole situation was leaving a bad taste in his mouth and it wouldn't go away.

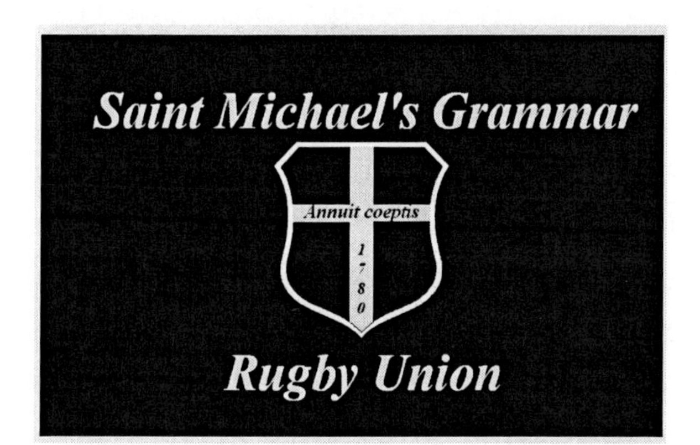

Saint Michael's

Saturday's bus trip to Saint Michael's Grammar had brought up feelings of mixed emotions for Bootsie, this was to be his first game for Charlton Hall and even though he wasn't named in the first 15 he had at least been given a spot on the bench for the game. The trip to the away school was very similar to an All Kings trip. The rugby boys and staff in one bus leading the way and a travelling circus of boys crammed into buses following behind. The usual sea of green, yellow and black streamers was replaced with Charlton Hall's familiar colours of red, white and navy blue and for the first time since his arrival at the school, Bootsie started to really miss All Kings. It was an unusual feeling when he pulled on the Charlton Hall jumper for the first time. He had been at the school for over four months but still didn't feel like he was a part of the place. Maybe it was the fact that he would only be here for a year and then he would be back at All Kings, playing for the school he felt he really belonged to.

Charlton Hall's rugby team had two jumpers that they used, a home jumper and an away jumper. Because today was an away game at Saint Michael's Grammar, the boys would be wearing the mostly white-coloured top. Home or away didn't matter to Bootsie because when he pulled on the top, the colours weren't green, black and yellow, so it felt strange. He would have to put his feelings aside for today and play his best for his new school. It wouldn't be fair on his teammates if he didn't put in 100% effort and contribute to the team.

With his heavily strapped ankle Bootsie walked out to the unwelcoming reception coming from the mostly

•

Saint Michael's supporters who had lined the sidelines of the field. He took his place on some seats that were positioned just to the left of the halfway line on the Charlton Hall supporters' side of the field. Some things are the same the world over and fanatical support for the school team was one thing that was certainly the same. Just like at an All Kings game the crowd was huge, and full of voice. Bootsie looked over at Ox who was wearing his familiar number 8 jumper and wondered if he would ever make the first 15 team this year. He was happy enough to at least be a reserve player today but warming the bench was something he didn't take kindly to, he knew he was a first 15 player and that's what he wanted to be at Charlton Hall as well.

Saint Michael's was a good opposition for the first game of the new season;

it was also a proud rugby school and had come third in the competition last year. Their school colours of yellow and black were repeated in the yellow and black stripes of their rugby jumpers. These were teamed with black shorts and black socks sporting yellow piping round their top edges. On the top left of their jumpers was a black shield with a yellow cross in the middle, with the school's motto embroidered on it. It said *Annuit coeptis,* which means 'God has favoured us' and below this were the numbers 1780, which was the year the school was founded. From the opening whistle their school motto was true, God was favouring them, well something was. Even the bounce of the ball was against the boys from Charlton Hall for the first half of the game and after only twenty minutes the score was Saint Michael's 17, Charlton Hall 0.

Having played the game since he was six, Bootsie could spot a weakness in any team. For Charlton Hall it was the left-winger, a boy called Lenny wearing the number 11. Bootsie spotted it and Saint Michael's must have noticed it as well because each time they got the ball they would attack his side of the field. Lenny was a really nice boy but unfortunately he was a bad rugby player. Cricket was his main game but during the rugby season turned his hand to the hard man's game. Well he tried to anyway, as a rugby player he made a great cricketer. His tackling ability was really letting the team down and Bootsie thought to himself that if *he* was playing for Saint Michael's he would be charging at Lenny every chance he got.

"Our backs are letting us down again," Charlie said to Bootsie as he sat next to him on the bench.

"Well one of them anyway," replied Bootsie.
"Good cricket player, not such a good rugby player," added Charlie.
"So you *do* know the game." Bootsie said to Charlie, who simply just smiled back at him.
"Maybe we should get you out there?" continued Bootsie.
"I wish," replied Charlie, "The Coach doesn't like me at all."
"Really, why?" asked a very curious Bootsie.
"Oh, my dad and him have got issues with each other about something that happened years ago," he replied.
"Really? What happened?" asked Bootsie, intrigued.
"I don't know the whole story. You can ask him later if you want. He's in the grandstand, never misses a game. I'll introduce you to him afterwards." he replied.

By half time the score had blown out to Saint Michael's 29, Charlton Hall 3. Bootsie sat in the change rooms and listened to the coach's half-time speech to the team. As the coach spoke to the players Bootsie noticed how dirty the white away tops were on the players who had taken the field in the first half. He looked down at his pristine white top and only hoped he would get a run in the second half. Amazingly Lenny still ran out to start the second half and once again Saint Michael's attacked his side of the field. Bootsie wondered to himself if this was the reason they had finished on the bottom of the ladder last year, a weak left wing. Bootsie thought it was fair enough to give him a go and keep him in the team but if it's going to cost you the game each week then surely you have to change plans at some point, surely.

With ten minutes to go, the coach told Bootsie to get ready to go on. When Bootsie stood on the sideline his mixed feelings about playing for the school had all disappeared, he wanted to get out there and help the team as much as he could. He had trained extremely hard during the pre season and was in what he felt was the best condition he had ever been in before. With ten minutes to go it was Saint Michael's 39, Charlton Hall 3.

From the minute he stepped onto the field he made an impact on the game. His efforts in the gym had really helped and his tackling had stepped up another level. Saint Michael's continually attacked Lenny's side of the field and Bootsie would break off the back of any scrums or rucks and always head left. In the ten minutes he played, Lenny didn't have to tackle anyone, as Bootsie would always cut

them off before they got anywhere near Lenny.
"Surely Ox should have been doing this," Bootsie thought to himself. Once Saint Michael's realised they had lost their attacking opportunity, the team folded. It was however all too late for Charlton Hall and even though they pegged back two converted tries, the final score was Saint Michael's 39, Charlton Hall 17.

Charlie was the first one to come and tell Bootsie he had played a good ten minutes.
"Come and meet my dad," he said to Bootsie. The boys walked over to the grandstand and on the way the Saint Michael's coach patted Bootsie on his back and said with a smile, "Lucky you only played 10 minutes." Bootsie headed to the grandstand with Charlie leading the way.

“Hey, that’s…” said Bootsie.
“Hi Dad,” Charlie said to the man in front of them.
“Hello son,” replied his dad as he gave Charlie a huge hug. “I take it he’s still not letting you play?” he asked his son.
“No, but its okay,” replied Charlie.
“Rubbish!” said his dad. “You and I both know the only reason he doesn’t let you play is because of what’s in the past between us,” he added.

Charlie’s dad glanced over at Bootsie. “Are you okay?’ he asked Bootsie who was looking a little bit stunned. “Y, y, yes,” he stammered back. “Aren’t you, like the greatest winger this country’s ever seen?” he asked.
“Well I don’t know about the greatest,” Charlie’s dad replied with a grin. “You played a great ten minutes, son. That damn stubborn coach of yours

will lose every game again this season with his son on the wing again," said Charlie's dad.
"His son?" replied a confused Bootsie.

Bootsie had kept his rugby skills a secret from Charlie until the last minute and Charlie had kept secrets of his own as well. What Charlie hadn't told Bootsie was his dad was a test legend, even Bootsie knew who he was. He was one of the country's greatest wingers and always played at number 11. Towards the end of his career he was benched to make way for a much younger, fitter and flashy new player. That new flashy player was the head coach at Charlton Hall and Lenny was the coach's son. The coach had only had limited success at the top level and was soon dropped for Charlie's dad again. He claimed at the time that he wasn't given enough time to show what he could really do,

which seemed very similar to today's situation.
"Ever seen Charlie's side-step?" Charlie's dad asked Bootsie.
"Sort of," he replied.
"Wicked it is, taught him myself," he added. "Bootsie it was nice to meet you and I'll see you boys again next week," he said as he shook hands with Bootsie, then said goodbye to his son before leaving.

7

Beginners Luck

By the time the boys said goodbye to Charlie's dad and Bootsie introduced Charlie to *his* parents they nearly missed the bus home to Charlton Hall. Bootsie also missed his chance to shower at the ground and would have to wait until he got back to Charlton Hall. Once they got back to school Bootsie showered, got changed and went down to Charlie's cubicle.

"C'mon Charlie explain yourself," he said to Charlie.

"Hey you had your secret and that was mine," he replied.

"So your dad's a test legend and you can actually play?" Bootsie asked him.

"I tried out for the first year but once the coach found out who my dad was, I had no chance," he replied. "In my dad's last test match he started on the bench and when he came on he replaced our coach because he had played so bad. In the papers the next day our coach was crucified by the press and it said something about even the tackling of an aging test legend was better than this supposed new whiz kid. He hated my dad from that day and I guess it's his way of getting revenge on my dad by taking it out on me and not letting me play," added Charlie.

Bootsie looked over at his friend and was gutted.
"This poor boy is made to suffer because the coach's feelings were hurt by the press one day and to make himself feel better he takes it out on Charlie when he had nothing to do with any of it," Bootsie thought to himself.
"Charlie, tomorrow we are starting a whole new training program," said Bootsie.
"We are?" replied Charlie.

“We are going to show the coach how this school needs a new winger and we’ve got the boy right here,” added Bootsie.
“What? You want to play on the wing now? What about Ox and the number 8 spot?” Charlie asked Bootsie.
“Not me. You!” replied Bootsie. “It is my new goal to get you into the team and too bad for Lenny but we’ll never win a game with *him* on the wing,” added Bootsie.
Charlie had a tear in his eye as he looked up at Bootsie.
“You would do that for me?” he asked Bootsie.
“Not just for you but for your dad as well,” replied Bootsie in a very fired-up voice.

Bootsie was true to his word. He usually used Sunday mornings as a sleep-in day at All Kings but the following Sunday morning he was

up early and standing at the end of Charlie's bed. He gave it a kick.
"Get up Charlie, we've got work to do," he said. Charlie threw off his blankets and was already dressed, including his running shoes.
"I wasn't sure if you really meant it," he said to Bootsie.
"Oh don't worry, I meant every word of it," replied Bootsie. "Me and your new friend pain are going to do everything we can to get you into the team. It's a promise," added Bootsie.
Charlie leapt out of his bed.
"Let's go then," he said.
"After you, my friend" replied Bootsie.

The boys went to the gym and put in a huge weights session before filling themselves with a massive breakfast in the dining hall. Bootsie continued to tell Charlie about his plan to get him onto the team and wasn't going to stop until he had.

“The coach really doesn’t like me,” Charlie said to Bootsie.
“Yeah, but if you give him no other options he has to play you,” replied Bootsie. “If you can show him at training that you’re ten times the winger that his son is, surely he can’t ignore that,” he added. As Bootsie sat and told Charlie of his plan, one of the senior boys came over to him and said, “There’s a spare seat on the rugby boys’ table for you now.” “What about Charlie, is there a seat for him?” asked Bootsie.
“Yeah good one, the tables are for players, not water boys,” said the senior boy.
“Oh I see. So he’s good enough to bring you the water each week but he can’t sit next to you in the dining hall,” replied Bootsie.
“I don’t make the rules, that’s just the way it is here. These tables are for *players* only,” responded the senior

boy. Bootsie looked the boy in the eyes and said, "Well I'll tell you what, how about you make room for two seats at that table because in no time at all the junior boys are going to have another new player. OK?"

The senior boy was totally shocked and stood in stunned silence; no player had ever refused to sit with the rugby boys before.
"Hey if you want to sit here then you go right ahead," he finally said to Bootsie.
"I'm not trying to be rude but Charlie is my friend and I'm *not* going to *not* sit next to him anymore just because *he* doesn't play in the team *yet*," replied Bootsie.
"I like your loyalty to your friend. It's commendable," said the senior boy to Bootsie before he returned to his table. When he'd sat down at his table again, you could see the discussion about

what had just happened overtake all other conversations on the rugby boys' table.

"Are you mad?" Charlie asked Bootsie. "One of the senior rugby boys sets a seat aside for you at their table and you turn him down. For me?" he added.
"Charlie, the day I sit at that table is the day you sit next to me at it," replied Bootsie.
"OK, I just hope you know what you're doing," added Charlie.
"No, it's what *we're* doing Charlie," replied Bootsie with a smile.
After the boys had eaten, Bootsie was awarded his first Charlton Hall rugby cap along with one other boy at a presentation in the dining hall. The headmaster gave him a very firm handshake when he handed him his new cap and proceeded to tell the

whole school about Bootsie being a former student at All Kings and how he was pleased to have him on the team this year. He also said how the school was looking forward to playing against the All Kings team, which was arriving at Charlton Hall in two weeks.

It was great for Bootsie to have a new focus and to take his mind off the imminent visit of the All Kings team. His new goal was to get Charlie into the junior boys team and as long as Charlie was willing, nothing was going to stop him. During the early part of the evening the two boys went down to the rugby grounds to train some more. Bootsie wanted to put Charlie through his paces to see what he really had to offer the team.
"Okay Charlie, lets see this wicked side step your dad taught you," Bootsie asked. "I'll stand here and you see if you can get past me," he added.

"Okay then," replied Charlie, as he grabbed the ball and ran about twenty metres away from where Bootsie was standing.
"Are you ready?" he asked Bootsie before he began his run towards him.
"Just start running at me," Bootsie firmly replied.
Charlie started his run and Bootsie moved up on him and readied himself for the tackle. Bootsie went to grab Charlie, but found himself tackling the air. Charlie was around him in a flash and made Bootsie look ordinary to say the least.
"Beginners luck," said a slightly embarrassed Bootsie as he got to his feet. "Do it again," he added.
Charlie tried again
"What was it that time?" asked Charlie who had put the ball down on the try line and was looking back at Bootsie who was on the ground. Again!

"So you've always been this good and the coach has always overlooked you?" asked a very puzzled Bootsie.
"As I said before, he hates my dad and I get punished for it," replied Charlie. "When I tried out in my first year for the junior team, he just told me I was too small and he would never put me in the team. I didn't even bother last year or this year. It's funny, my dad said he was always told *he* was too small to play at international level but once he cracked the team he never heard it again," he added.
"Can you tackle?" asked Bootsie.
"Try me," replied Charlie.
"Ooh confidence. I like that," added Bootsie as he walked over and took the ball from Charlie.

The boys swapped roles and Bootsie charged at Charlie with the ball in hand. Charlie wrapped his arms

around Bootsie's legs and Bootsie hit the ground, *hard.*
"Beginners luck was it?" asked Charlie sarcastically.
"No that was just a good tackle," replied a shocked Bootsie. "You've got talent, so much talent and it's sitting on the sidelines and carrying water each week. It's ridiculous," said a frustrated Bootsie. "We've somehow got to make the coach have no alternative but to put you on the team," added Bootsie.
"Well, I don't know how you're going to do it," said a curious Charlie.
"How *we* are going to do it Charlie, how *we* are going to do it," replied Bootsie.

Bootsie wasn't quite sure yet how he was going to get his friend onto the team. The head coach certainly wasn't going to just drop his son to make way for Charlie, because if he was, it would have happened already. Last year Lenny had played in every game for Charlton Hall except for the tour to Bluedale and All Kings, in fact he missed the entire trip due to an appendix operation. When Charlie told Bootsie about the operation it made something click in Bootsie's head.

"You know I think I know how to get the ball rolling," he said to Charlie.

"How?" asked a very interested Charlie.

"Just leave it with me my little side-stepping friend. I think I've got the answer to all our problems," replied Bootsie.

The Plan

The key to Bootsie's plan working all depended on the coach's son Lenny; if he was receptive to Bootsie's idea, then his crazy scheme might just work. He wasn't asking too much, just step aside and let Charlie ease his way into the team. As Bootsie walked to Lenny's dormitory to put forward his idea, he had an uncomfortable feeling about what he was going to say to him when he got there. What he *did* find was a very shy and quiet boy, Lenny was completely the opposite of what Bootsie had expected. Charlie had told him that Lenny was probably the best cricket player the school had ever seen and with this information Bootsie was expecting a big-headed arrogant boy, but when he sat down and spoke with Lenny he got the total opposite.

Bootsie sat stunned as Lenny told him how much he hated rugby.

"My dad makes me play, I hate the game," he said to Bootsie. "Just because my dad played he expects me to follow in his footsteps but I just don't like the game. I hate playing in the wet, I can't tackle and I'm scared I'll get injured and never be able to play cricket again which is the sport I really love and I'm actually good at," he added to a very quiet Bootsie.
"Have you told your dad about this?" asked Bootsie.
"Many times. He just doesn't listen, he just tells me I'm weak or I'm soft. You'd think he'd be pleased about the cricket but he doesn't like the game just like I don't like rugby and he hardly ever comes to watch me play," replied Lenny.

When Bootsie first thought up his plan he knew it all hinged on Lenny, but what he wasn't expecting was how open Lenny was to the idea. "Bootsie if I never play another game of rugby I'll be very happy and if you can help this happen you can count on me to help. I have heard my dad talk about Charlie's dad many, many times. He told me not to even be his friend, which I could never understand why. I knew it had something to do with his dad but he never told me the whole story. I just respected his wishes and always went out of my way to avoid Charlie. It sounds terrible because Charlie seems really nice but I really love my dad even though he forces me to play each season," continued Lenny.

Bootsie's astonishment at this confession soon turned to action as he laid out his plan to Lenny who was all ears.
"Easy, I can do that. No problems at all," he said to Bootsie.

"Good, good, but this is between me and you okay? Charlie mustn't know anything about it. He *is* good enough to be in the team but without your help, and as long as your dad is coaching, he's got no chance," replied Bootsie. The two boys shook hands on the deal and said goodbye to one another.

Saturday's game was at home against another local school, Saint Stephens. If Bootsie wanted to get Charlie into the team he would have put his plan into action today. Charlie was still unaware of what he had conjured up in order to execute his mission. Charlie thought something was up when Bootsie made him put on a Charlton Hall jumper.
"Here put this old one on, number 23," he said to Charlie in the changing rooms before the game.
"Why?" asked Charlie.

"Just put it on and worry about it later," replied Bootsie. The atmosphere at Charlton Hall was pretty intense to say the least. They had massive home support at the ground and the grandstand was packed with old boys in their school caps. Once again Bootsie was on the bench despite his efforts last week and Ox was again at his usual number 8 starting position.

Not that Bootsie thought he was better than Ox but when he came on last week he stopped the barrage of tries against Charlton Hall and had helped set up the two late tries his team scored. He did feel a little disappointed that he was going to miss out on the starting 15 again and it would probably stay this way all year. It was fairly wet and miserable on the Saturday the two teams met and as far as ball handling went, it was an ugly encounter. Scrums were set and reset due to handling errors and knock ons, all the extra work was showing on the forward pack and soon the coach was going to have to make some changes. Bootsie couldn't tell if Lenny was trying to get dropped from the team or he was just really that bad at tackling, but he had let a stream of Saint Stephen's attackers through his defence and the half-time score was Saint Stephens 28, Charlton Hall 6.

Bootsie listened to the half-time address from his coach and once again he felt he had completely misjudged what was going wrong out there. Each time there was a scrum set, Saint Stephens would play the ball to their right and Ox couldn't come off the back of the rucks and scrums fast enough to help cover in defence. He wasn't the only one who was missing tackles but last week Bootsie had picked up what was happening and when he had replaced Ox he had single-handidly put a stop to it. Once again, this week, the opposition was exploiting the weaker side of the field. Finally with only ten minutes to go and many more tries scored against them Bootsie was substituted for Ox. The big unit seemed to be limping slightly as he left the field and he wished Bootsie good luck as they ran past each other in different directions.

When Bootsie came onto the field, the entire bench was also put on with him due to there being so many injured players leaving the field and the game soon began to turn. Once the substitute players took the field the rest of the game was played inside the Saint Stephens' half of the field. One boy got two tries within five minutes of taking the field with two blistering runs through the centre and Bootsie got his first for the school when he barged through what he thought was a pretty weak defensive line late in the game. With only what must have been a minute to go the score was Saint Stephens 45, Charlton hall 23.

The referee told the boys it was the last minute of the game. Bootsie was deep inside his own half and made sure he took the high ball after the re-start. As he took off with the ball he could see Charlie on the sideline holding a water bottle in his hand. Bootsie pushed through the first tackler and found a gap; he took off up the wing, right next to the sideline where Charlie was standing. As the defenders bore down on him he could see he had no option but to pass the ball, but instead of passing inside the field he passed the ball out to Charlie who wasn't even playing *and* he was holding a water bottle *and* wearing tracksuit pants! Charlie caught the

ball and was still able to hang onto the water bottle he was carrying.
"RUN CHARLIE!" Bootsie screamed, and that's what Charlie did. He was wearing a Charlton Hall rugby top and most of the Saint Stephens boys were unaware what was going on and furiously tried to stop what they thought was just another player from Charlton Hall. Charlie stepped onto the field on the Charlton Hall 22 metre line and ran the length of the field untouched. He sidestepped at least four defending players, dummy passed to two who both fell for it and by the time he was inside the Saint Stephens 22 he was all alone. Even the referee was still outside the 22. He had a clear run to the try line and put the ball down under the posts as well as the water bottle. When the referee arrived he put his hand up, blew his whistle and awarded Charlie the try.

That was until the touch judge or assistant referee as they are sometimes called came running up to him to tell him what he had missed. The slightly embarrassed referee blew his whistle and awarded a penalty to Saint Stephens way back down field. After the missed penalty attempt, he blew his whistle for the end of the game while most of the crowd was still laughing about what had just happened. It didn't matter what the score was, all that mattered was Bootsie's plan had worked and the whole school had seen how good Charlie really was.

His coach wasn't so pleased about what had just happened and tried to say Bootsie had passed to Charlie on purpose.
"What were you thinking?" he shouted at Bootsie as they stood on the sideline.

"I just saw the red, white and blue jumper beside me, so I passed," Bootsie sheepishly answered, knowing exactly what he had done.
"As for you," said to the coach to Charlie. "Well I'll.."
"Well you'll what?" said Charlie's dad who had made his way over to where the boys and coach were standing. "That was the best run this school's seen in two years and you won't give the boy a run because of something that happened between me and you a long time ago," snarled Charlie's dad to the coach.
"Just go and get showered you lot and we'll deal with this later," the coach said to the boys.

Bootsie and the rest of the team headed for the showers and left the coach and Charlie's dad still heatedly discussing their unfinished business from many years ago. Charlie was so excited about scoring the try and didn't care that it was disallowed. He had done something he had always dreamed of; a try for his school. As mad as the coach must have been, surely he must have seen the talent in Charlie today. No one who saw his run could deny that he was a gifted player, but only time would really tell.

9

All Kings

The fallout from Saturday's game wasn't overly bad and Charlie was summoned to the headmaster's office to explain his actions on Monday morning. He didn't care what his punishment was, he had felt like a caged tiger for the last two years and on Saturday afternoon he had been unleashed by Bootsie. The headmaster listened as Charlie told him a few things that I'm sure he had never heard before; he was quite shocked to hear about the history between the coach and Charlie's dad. Charlie's dad had been a student at Charlton Hall and despite being a test legend when he was younger he was still an old boy and wore his Charlton Hall cap to each home game with pride. It must have been very painful for him to never see his son play for the school and must have been why he had defended his son so strongly after Saturday's game.

The headmaster told Charlie he wasn't going to punish him any more for his actions on Saturday as he felt that Charlie had suffered enough. After his conversation with Charlie, the headmaster summoned the coach to his office. He denied all knowledge of what the headmaster had been told by Charlie of course and told the headmaster the reason why Charlie hadn't made the team was because of his small size, which was something the headmaster couldn't prove.

Whatever was said in the headmaster's office didn't take away from the fact that the first stage of Bootsie's master plan had worked a treat. What he hadn't planned on was what he and Charlie would have to face at training during the week. The coach was hard on both of them to say the least. He was especially hard on Charlie who wasn't even part of the playing team and only came to training, hoping one day to be given at least a spot on the bench one Saturday afternoon. It didn't bother Bootsie one bit that on Wednesday morning the All Kings boys would be arriving ahead of their game against Charlton Hall on Saturday. They were only playing each other once and then All Kings would move on and play a game against Saint Michael's as well.

When the bus arrived at the school the following morning Bootsie felt very excited and was part of the welcoming party sent to greet the headmaster and boys from All Kings. He stood next to his headmaster, coach and one of the senior boys and was the second one of the three to shake hands with his former headmaster as he stepped from the bus. "Young Bootsie, it's great to see you again," said his All

Kings headmaster. “I hope they’re treating you well here?” he asked. Bootsie stood and shook hands with each and every boy as they stepped down from the bus and onto the grounds of Charlton Hall. It felt great to see boys such as John, Socks and especially his good friend Razzi again. He was even more pleased when his All Kings coach stepped down from the bus. After not seeing him for so long Bootsie had forgotten how huge he was. When his All Kings coach shook hands with the Charlton Hall coach he even made him look tiny.

“What do you reckon about this place?” his old coach asked. Bootsie leaned over and in a quiet voice replied, “I can’t wait to get back to All Kings. I really miss the place, even the boy journalists.”
His former coach laughed at what Bootsie had just said to him.

“I’m sure you don’t miss them really,” he replied to Bootsie.
“Yeah, you’re probably right,” added Bootsie.
It was Bootsie’s job to show the All Kings boys around the college for the time they would spend at the school. The next time he saw his old friend Razzi, he was sticking his thumb in his mouth and blowing up his cheeks.
“Been hitting the weights Bootsie?” asked Razzi as his cheeks deflated.
“Yeah a bit,” replied Bootsie.
“A bit? You’re huge!” said Razzi.

“Now have you got any tips for us before Saturday’s game?” continued Razzi in his jovial voice.
“Attack our left wing!” Bootsie joked, trying to disguise that it was actually the truth and all part of his master plan.
“Why?” asked Razzi.

"The left winger can't tackle," replied Bootsie.
"What you mean? Don't tell me they've got you playing left wing over here?" laughed Razzi.
"Yeah, good one," replied Bootsie.

For the first time before a game Bootsie actually hoped he would be on the bench, he loved the game but he simply didn't want to play against his old school. It might have been different if he was staying permanently at Charlton Hall but he knew next year he would be back in his familiar colours and couldn't wait to get back to All Kings. When he was greeted by Charlie later in the day he was reminded by seeing him that he still had unfinished business here at Charlton Hall, that he had to take care of first, before he went anywhere.

Game day soon came around and as Bootsie sat in the change rooms and put on his familiar number 18 jumper, he felt a little better about the game now that it was finally here. Charlton Hall had special jumpers made for the day, each with a special logo sewn into it saying, 'All Kings V Charlton Hall Friendship Game'. It was expected that the boys would exchange jumpers at the end of the game and Bootsie would get to own a special All Kings jumper with a black number on the back. Even though it said 'Friendship Game' on the logo, the game was all but friendly. The last time the two teams had played it was quite a dirty encounter and today's game was beginning to look like it might end up the same way. The trouble was that Bootsie didn't really want to get in the middle of it this time. Razzi must have told the All Kings boys to try out the left wing's defence or lack of it and once they saw the weakness, they targeted it very effectively.

"Same as the last two weeks," Bootsie said to Charlie on the sidelines. "Yep, ever since he hurt his knee on last year's tour he can't step left," replied Charlie.
"Whoa what did you say?" asked Bootsie.
"Ox hurt his knee on the overseas tour last year. It wasn't against All Kings, it was the game before that but that's why you wouldn't have seen him play before you came here," replied Charlie. "You watch how slow he is when the play goes to our left after a scrum or breakdown," he added.
"Yeah, I already know. I sort of picked it up in the first game and watched him closely last week and noticed something was wrong with him," replied Bootsie.

"Here we go! All Kings have got it and if they play the ball to our left, yep, here they go, you watch Ox now. See, see. Did you see how slow he was?" said an excited Charlie.
"Yes I saw," replied Bootsie. "So who played on the wing on tour last year if Lenny was in hospital?" asked Bootsie.
"I think it was one of the senior boys who has moved up a grade this year," he replied.
"Must have been, because I can't remember a weakness like that wing last year and you guys smashed Bluedale and then beat us a week later," added Bootsie.

•

Late in the game Bootsie was thrown into the action. Even though it was *his* school he was really playing against, when he crossed the white line Bootsie played like he had never seen them before. He wanted to show his old coach he could still play and next year wanted a spot in the senior team. Unfortunately for Charlton Hall the All Kings boys had run through enough tries already to put the game out of reach and by the time Bootsie went onto the field, the score was very one sided. He peeled off the back of the scrum and was tackled by his old mate Razzi who wasn't holding anything back. As he went to get up, Razzi pushed Bootsie's head into the ground.

"Geez thanks a lot Razzi," Bootsie thought to himself as he wiped the extra mud from his face.

All in all it had been a good day and Bootsie ended up swapping his number 18 jumper for Razzi's number 7. He shook hands with his old friend and said, "Great game, but I'd much rather be on the same team as you next time. Oh yeah and thanks for

pushing my face into the mud over there as well," Bootsie added.
"Was that your head, err.. I mean I wouldn't have done a thing like that," was all Razzi replied with a large sheepish grin on his face.
It had been good to see so many of his friends from home and he couldn't wait to go home himself, but before he left Charlton Hall he had one more thing to take care of.

What a Year

The game against the All Kings team had really taken its toll on the Charlton Hall boys; Tuesday and Thursday nights' training was like a hospital. Without even being aware of it, the situation played nicely into Bootsie's master plan. The more injuries to the backs meant a higher chance that Charlie would finally get a game and Bootsie knew once he got to play a game there was no way the coach could ever deny him again. The problem was that Lenny was the most resilient player on the team and wasn't showing any signs of injury at all. It might have been due to the fact that he missed every tackle and didn't get into a lot of contact anyway but either way he was still fit and ready for Saturday.

Game day arrived and it meant a long travel to St Mark's Grammar which was a good distance away from

Charlton Hall. Bootsie sat on the main bus and once again Charlie had to ride on the buses with the other *non players* as further punishment for his try two weeks ago. They arrived at the very impressive grounds at St Mark's, which was a very nice school and had a good reputation as a hard rugby team. They had won the senior boys and junior boys competition last season and were expected to give Charlton Hall a touch up today. The main bus stopped in the grounds and the boys stood up in the aisle ready to get out. As Bootsie moved down towards the front of the bus he could hear something was happening outside.

When he finally got off the bus he could see Lenny hanging onto his ankle and grimacing in pain.
"Let's have a look," his dad said as he pulled his sock down slightly. "Wow,

that's turning purple already," he said as he looked at his injured son's leg. "Let's get some ice on that straight away," he added.
"What happened?" Bootsie asked one of the boys who saw what had happened.
"Lenny fell from the step and rolled his ankle, I think," he replied. "Ouch, I've done that. He won't be playing for a while," added Bootsie.

In the changing rooms before the game, the two coaches had a heated discussion about who would be playing where, now that Lenny was out and probably would be for at least a few weeks. The two coaches had to go into a separate room and shut the door to finish their heated debate. Even with the door closed the boys could hear their raised voices coming from the adjoining room. Most of the boys ran over and put their ears to the door in an attempt to hear what was being said. They all fell over backwards when the door was suddenly pushed open as the two coaches re-entered the main change room. Bootsie almost felt his insides explode when he heard what the assistant coach said next. "Charlie, kit-up. You're on the bench," he said as he reached into the bag of jumpers and threw him the number 22 jumper. Charlie almost couldn't contain himself; he was so pleased to be given this slight chance of playing.

Bootsie was stunned when he realized he had been given the number 8 jumper and Ox looked equally dumbfounded as he was handed number 18. Bootsie was at a loss to work out the assistant coach's sudden change of direction. Not that he minded though, this was what he had been working towards and knew today was the time to show how hard he had worked for this moment.

St Mark's grammar school colours were maroon and white. Their rugby strip was maroon jumpers with a white V on the front, white shorts and maroon and white socks. They had their school logo on their jumpers which was a maroon shield with a white V at the top. The school motto was *'Docendo discitur'* in Latin which means, 'It is learned by teaching'. The school was opened in 1932 and the Latin motto and the year 1932 were also sewn into the school logo on the jumper.

If as their school motto said, 'It is learned by teaching' then at St Mark's they must have had good teachers, rugby teachers anyway. They were in a class all of their own and Bootsie could only thank the fact that the left wing was now being defended by Christian who was much better in defence than Lenny. Actually Bootsie thought his own sister would be better in defence than Lenny. Ox was usually the captain of the team, but this week Bootsie was given that responsibility as well, and he loved it. He really took charge out on the field and directed his troops from behind the scrum, just like he had been told many years ago by a certain coach. Considering St Mark's had won the competition last year and Charlton Hall had come last, today was a much more even contest. The whole team knew their weak point had finally been plugged and shouldn't leak half as much today; this gave them a fighting chance from the beginning of the game. Bootsie managed to get over for a try just before half time and at the half-time break the score was finally a respectable one. Charlton Hall 7, St Mark's 9.

It was quite strange at half time when only the assistant coach came into the changing rooms and gave the speech to the players; he was much calmer in his address than the usual coach and seemed to get a much more positive response from the players. By the time the boys took to the field for the start of the second half there was finally some belief in the team that they could go on and finally win a game. Bootsie put in all his efforts that day for his adopted school and for the first time since he got there, felt like a part of the place. His efforts had really made a difference and they were soon ahead on the scoreboard, Charlton Hall 14, St Mark's 9.

The assistant coach looked over to his substitute players and said, "Charlie you're up. Charlie did you hear me? I said you're up,"

"Sorry, I thought I imagined it," Charlie replied. "Are you serious?" Charlie asked again.
"Yes Charlie. Get your tracksuit off and get out there," the assistant coach replied.
Charlie jumped up from his chair and in his hurry to get his tracksuit bottoms off, got one of the legs stuck to his boot and he fell over onto the pile of water bottles nearby.
"Oops!" he said as he picked his wet body up from the pile of squashed plastic bottles that had imploded on his impact.
"Come on Charlie, get out there and take the left wing," said the coach, who had taken off the inside centre and moved another boy into that spot which freed up the left wing for a very, very excited Charlie.
"Please Charlie, make this count," Bootsie thought to himself as he

looked over at his best friend on the wing.

As soon as the Charlton Hall boys took the ball from the restart it was fed out to Charlie on the wing and from his opening touch he was electric to watch. He was a force all unto his own from the moment he took the field. No player could get near him and he cut the defence to pieces like a ribbon. From that first restart he side stepped two defenders to put the ball down under the black dot without another player anywhere near him to try and stop him. He even stood there for a moment, looked into the crowd, kissed the ball and then finally grounded it.

At the time he wouldn't have known it but when Charlie put that ball down, tears were streaming down his dad's face as he watched from the sidelines.

He'd had no idea that his son would even be taking the field today. How proud he must have been when he watched his son run in his second, then third, then fourth try for the day. What was expected to be a one-sided game had certainly lived up to that expectation except it was totally the other way, by the end of the game the final score was Charlton Hall 56, St Mark's 9.

Bootsie ran over and hugged his little champion winger; he was so pleased for him that he didn't let him go. They were soon joined by the rest of the team who were so ecstatic that they had won their first game in a long time. Charlie's dad soon joined the boys and hugged his son until Charlie thought he might pass out from lack of oxygen as his dad was squeezing so tight. What a day for the two boys as well as the rest of the team. The bus trip back to Charlton Hall was rowdier than it had been for some time, and Charlie was the first one onto the player's bus and he went to and from every away game in it for the rest of the season.

The following morning after breakfast Charlie was awarded his first cap by a very excited headmaster, even his dad was invited to the presentation and looked on with so much pride as his son was finally given what he had deserved for so long. The captain of the senior boys came over to Bootsie and Charlie and pointed to two empty seats at the rugby boys table and together the two boys took their place alongside all the other rugby boys.

Charlie had changed into a new boy since the day Bootsie had sat next to him on the first evening in the dining hall. He was now a rugby boy and he

knew Bootsie had a lot to do with it and he probably couldn't ever thank him enough. What Charlie didn't know was how *much* Bootsie had to do with it. Lenny didn't roll his ankle when he stepped down from the bus at St Mark's, it was all an act prearranged between Bootsie and Lenny the first time Bootsie went to see him about his master plan.
The two of them sat up late on Friday night painting Lenny's ankle, trying to make it look like how Bootsie's ankle looked when he rolled it playing for the Bulldogs.

They must have done a good job because he had everyone convinced for weeks and it got him out of playing for the rest of the year. Lenny's dad stepped down as the senior coach on Monday morning and the assistant coach led the boys for the rest of the year. They eventually finished in second place, which was a lot better than where they had been in the previous year. Charlie was given and hung onto the number 11 jumper for the rest of the year and ended up being the leading try scorer for the competition.

Before Bootsie was really ready, it was time for him to leave Charlton Hall and return to his real home at All Kings. The week before the end of the school year he was given a plaque by the school in recognition of his efforts on the rugby field. The school had actually grown on him more than he had been prepared for; when he packed his things to leave, he didn't realize how much he was going to miss the place. His Charlton Hall blazer and rugby cap would always remind him of the time he had spent at Charlton Hall and his All Kings jumper with a black number 7 on the back was also a special memento of his time here. One thing he found he hadn't prepared for was saying goodbye to Charlie. Bootsie had changed his life forever and Charlie didn't know how he could ever thank him for that. It was hard for the two boys to say goodbye when the time came and Charlie told Bootsie he was his friend for life and would always be in touch with him, no matter how far apart their schools were.

The time he had spent at Charlton Hall had matured Bootsie into a young man. What a year it had been for him. So much had happened that it felt like he had spent *two* years there instead of one. He was sad about leaving his adopted school and some very close friends he had made there, especially Charlie. But, he was already looking forward to returning to his old school, even as he looked back at Charlton

Hall when his parents drove him away for the last time. Who knew *what* would happen when he returned to All Kings? Certainly not Bootsie, because if he did, he might have wished he'd stayed at Charlton Hall!

The End.

Check out the Bootsie website
www.bootsiebooks.com

Thanks to KooGa Rugby
www.kooga.com.au

Lightning Source UK Ltd.
Milton Keynes UK
UKOW02f0915231115

263324UK00001B/56/P